Seal Island

SCHOOL

ISBN 0-439-19267-6

12 11 10 9 8 7 6 5 4 3   3 4 5/0

Printed in the U.S.A.   40

First Scholastic printing, November 2000

Set in OptiBaskerville

For Ben and Sarah who also made wishes.
—S. B.

Seal Island
SCHOOL

by Susan Bartlett

illustrated by Tricia Tusa

SCHOLASTIC INC.

New York Toronto London Auckland Sydney
Mexico City New Delhi Hong Kong

CONTENTS

CHAPTER ONE

The Best Teacher in Maine

A skinny tail poked from under the top of Pru Stanley's desk.

"Is that *alive*?" Miss Sparling stared at the tail.

"It's my gerbil, Jingle," said Pru. "I brought him to show Doug and Max." Doug Miller and Max Day were the two first graders in the Seal Island school.

The teacher smiled. "Can you wait until lunchtime?"

"Okay. I'll put him in the wastebasket where he can't get out." Outside the wind blew sleet against the windows. "I carried him in my pocket to keep him warm."

Pru was sure that Miss Sparling was the best teacher in Maine. She was certainly the prettiest. Pru wanted to grow her hair long like Miss Sparling's. Right now it was short and curly.

Maybe I should give her the gerbil, Pru thought. She says that she loves animals. Pru wanted Miss Sparling to like Seal Island so much she'd stay forever. Each year a different teacher came to the two-room school. Each year the teacher left in June. "It's lonely here," they said. It didn't seem

lonely to Pru. Forty-nine people lived on the island. That was plenty of friends.

Pru had grown up with Doug and Max, and with Harry and Hannah. Harry Smith was in fifth grade and Hannah Spencer in sixth. Almost everyone lived along the harbor's edge where the houses stood close together against the wind and spray. Almost everyone except Harry. He lived on the top of Cemetery Hill.

From Harry's hill, Pru liked to count the houses in the village. She knew who lived in each one. And she knew who owned each lobster boat in the harbor. Trapping and selling lobsters was the way most families made a living. The only cars were three old pickups, which the lobstermen used for hauling gear and supplies. Pru and her dog Schooner could walk everywhere.

Pru set the gerbil gently in the wastebasket and walked back to her desk. Through the windows she saw the waves foam against Gull Rock, black and ice-covered in the harbor. The sleet turned to snow.

"Book time," said Miss Sparling. "You're doing so

well. You'll soon be reading the *New York Times*."

"Is that a book I'd like?" asked Doug.

"That's a newspaper," Nicholas explained. "My newspaper."

Nicholas Lansing-Ross was new to the school and the only fourth grader. His parents had just come to Maine from New York City. "They thought it would be great to live on an island for the winter," Nicholas had told Pru. "Of course, no one asked *me*."

Pru and Nicholas moved to a corner to read while Miss Sparling listened to Doug and Max. "How come you've got two last names?" Pru asked.

"It's my mother's and father's names put together. My mom's a feminist. She didn't want to give up her name when she got married."

"I don't think I will either," Pru said, though she wasn't sure what a feminist was. "You know lots of big words."

"I read a lot. And I have a photographic memory. Like my mom."

Nicholas's mother was a painter. Pru had seen one of her paintings, called "Winter Storm."

It looked like someone had smeared blobs of blue and green on a rock. Pru didn't think it was photographic at all.

"My mom invited Miss Sparling over for supper tomorrow." Pru liked to think the teacher was her special friend.

Nicholas whispered, "She doesn't like it here."

"No way!" Pru was startled. "You're just saying that because *you* don't like it."

"She told my mom that she gets claustrophobia."

"What's that?" asked Pru.

"It means you feel trapped," said Nicholas. "My mom says it's psychological."

"But she can go ashore."

"Yeah, but in winter the boat doesn't run weekends, and school days she has to be here."

Outdoors, the swirling flakes hid the flagpole in the schoolyard. The room grew darker. Miss Sparling flipped a switch to start the generator. The motor rumbled and chugged and the lights blinked on. The island was too far from the mainland to have electricity, so the school made its own. Most families had gas lights.

"Pru and Nicholas, do I hear reading?" Miss Sparling called. "It doesn't sound like *Sarah, Plain and Tall* to me."

"Did Mama sing every day?" Pru read quickly. "Every-single-day?"

Yes, Pru thought, she'd definitely ask Miss Sparling whether she wanted Jingle. With a pet in her house, Miss Sparling couldn't get lonesome. And maybe it would even help that claustrophobia.

CHAPTER TWO

Surprise from the Sea

The sky was blue as a jay feather when Pru left the house. She liked to walk along the shore before school. "Hello, Flipper," she said to a seal as it slid from Gull Rock into the water. The thin layer of snow had melted, and her boots made damp prints in the sand.

The lobstermen had left the harbor before sunrise. The sea was quiet for the first time in many days. All week the wind had blown hard from the northeast and high waves had made it too dangerous to check the lobster traps.

Pru looked down at the sand. Once she'd found

an eider duck's nest, lined with soft, gray feathers. There were always crab and mussel shells, and sometimes lobster buoys still tied to pieces of line. Maybe she'd find something for Miss Sparling, who hadn't wanted the gerbil after all.

"Thank you, Pru," she said. "That's very nice. I know how much you like Jingle. But I'm saving my money for a Newfoundland."

"I thought Newfoundland was a place."

"It is," said Miss Sparling. "Big, shaggy dogs come from there. They're good company."

"Are you lonesome?" Pru had to know.

But then Doug and Max began to throw crayons, and Miss Sparling had not answered.

Pru saw a bit of green glass half hidden under a piece of driftwood. She bent over to pry it out. It was a bottle, sticky with salt from the sea. Something moved inside. It looked like paper. All rolled up. Pru tried to pull out the cork, but it was stuck tight.

She hugged the bottle to her parka and ran up the path to school. Miss Sparling was on the steps in her jogging suit. She often jogged early in the morn-ing—from the little house she was renting beyond the store to the dock and back again. Sometimes she ran right to school.

"Look what I've got!" Pru called.

"Hi, early bird." Miss Sparling held the door open for Pru and they went inside. "What is it?"

Pru caught her breath and held up the bottle. "Can you help me open it?"

Miss Sparling twisted off the cork. Pru took out the paper and spread it on her desk. There was a message in red marker. Pru read as Miss Sparling looked over her shoulder:

To someone on Seal Island,
I hope you find this letter. I am sending it by sea.
I like to pretend I'm on a sailing ship, like my
great-great-grandmother. Her father was the
captain. My dad showed me Seal Island on a map. I
wish I lived on an island.
      Please write back.
            Clara Hall
            Shore Road
            Cranberry Cove, Maine
 P.S. I'm eight years old and in the third grade. I
have a cat named Clam.

"Wow!" said Pru. "A letter in a bottle!"

"It only happens in books." Nicholas stood in the door. The rest of the children were behind him. It was time for school to start.

"Well, it's happened here," said Miss Sparling. "Pru's found a treasure."

"Let's write back today," said Pru after everyone heard the news.

Hannah Spencer groaned. She hated to write letters.

"How shall we send it?" asked Miss Sparling.

"By U.S. mail," said Harry, whose father was the postmaster. "So it will get there fast."

Dear Clara,
Pru found your bottle on the beach. Now we
have to write you. I have my own flat-
bottomed dory. I like to run. I won the 100-
yard dash at a track meet in Portland.
Harry Smith

I painted my nails purple, but my mom won't
let me wear lipstick. How many in your
school? I wish someone else was in my
grade. I am IT. I am also the only kid
with TV. That's because my dad bought a
generator. And a TV!
Hannah Spencer

I was extremely surprised to get a letter
in a bottle. The chances of it reaching our
island seemed slim. Still, I am glad that it
did.
Nicholas Lansing-Ross

I was in Cranberry Cove once. I saw the lighthouse. We play hockey on the ice pond. I am goalie. We have the best teacher ever. She plays hockey and she likes big dogs.
Your friend, Pru Stanley
P. S. I'm in third grade, too.

I have a ferret. His name is Ferocious.
Max

I collect feathers and fish bones. I have 22 feathers. One from a puffin.
Doug

From Seal Island School.
Miss Sparling, Teacher

At recess time they all walked down Main Street to the post office. The only street on the island was more like a wide path. Perfect for riding a pony, Pru thought for the umpteenth time. The path went from the dock where the ferry arrived past the inn where the summer people stayed to the post office, the church, and the general store.

Miss Sparling bought a stamp, and Pru dropped the envelope in the box outside the door. Tomorrow the boat would take it across the water to Rockland. Maybe they'd hear back soon.

Pru was sure Miss Sparling liked adventure. So much was happening. Who would want to leave Seal Island? Especially since another special day was coming so soon.

CHAPTER THREE

The Fantastic Field Trip

"Happy birthday!" Pru's parents pushed open the school door. It was February 28. Her dad carried a birthday cake with nine red candles. He and Mom had on paper hats with silver stars, and Mom held nine balloons.

"Are those dogs on the cake?" asked Nicholas.

Dad set the cake on Miss Sparling's desk.

"That's Schooner," said Pru, pointing to her dog. "And there's Picasso." Nicholas's poodle was outlined in brown frosting.

"I see my dog," Max said. "You're a good drawer, Mrs. Stanley."

"How come you didn't draw my rabbit?" Doug asked.

"It's a canine cake," said Pru's father. "Only dogs this time. Next time we'll do rabbits." He stuck out his front teeth and made a rabbit face at Doug.

"My mom's the best baker ever." Pru's mother baked breads, pies, and cookies for the summer people when she wasn't writing articles about the island for the *Ellsworth News*. People stopped by the house with their orders. Usually Mom invited them to have a cup of coffee and a hot muffin.

"There go your profits," Dad sometimes said. But Pru knew Mom cared more about her friends than money.

Max stuck his fingers in the frosting and licked them.

"Food later." Mom covered the cake with plastic wrap. "First, we're going to meet the boat."

"How come?" asked Pru.

"Class field trip." Miss Sparling waved them toward the door.

Pru led the way down the path to the harbor. The boat chugged around Gull Rock, then cut its engine and coasted up to the dock. Twelve o'clock. Right on time.

"Hi, birthday girl!" called Captain Hill. He tossed Pru a line, and she hitched it fast to a piling.

"Stand back," Dad ordered. Chains rattled and the gangplank slid into place.

Pru stared. Something brown and shaggy moved on the deck. It was tied to the rail. Maybe it was that dog Miss Sparling wanted. Then she heard it whinny.

It was a pony. A real, live pony!

Mom and Dad began to sing "Happy Birthday to You."

Pru looked at her mom and then at her dad. Did they mean the pony was for *her*? Captain Hill led the pony down the gangplank and handed Pru the lead rope.

"It's your birthday present," Mom said. "His name is Velvet."

The pony shook himself and whinnied again. He looked at Pru with chocolate eyes. "He's beautiful." Pru reached out to touch him. "Thank you, I mean, wow, thanks a zillion!" The pony nibbled her fingers. "He's biting me!"

"He's curious," Dad said. "Just keep your hand flat."

"Where did he come from?" asked Pru.

"Portland," Mom said. "His owner outgrew him and wanted him to go to a good home."

Pru thought she must be dreaming. Her very own pony? She patted the pony's neck. He certainly felt real. "How did he get on the boat?"

"A friend trucked him to Rockland and loaded him. Captain Hill helped us work it out." Dad shook Captain Hill's hand and thanked him.

"Fantastic!" Hannah said. "There's never been a pony here before."

"My great-grandfather had a horse," Mom remembered. "I've seen pictures."

"But that was ages ago." Hannah took off one woolen mitten and touched a finger to Velvet's black nose. "I meant since I was born."

"Can I hug him?" Max went closer and stopped. "He's got big teeth."

"Superexcellent!" said Nicholas. "I don't know anyone in New York who has a pony."

"What will he eat?" Harry looked at the ground. "There's no grass."

"You'll see." Captain Hill headed back up the gangplank. "My boat can deliver anything, even pony food." Pru's mom and dad walked on board and began to unload bales of hay. Everyone except Pru, who held Velvet's lead rope tightly, took turns carrying the hay to one of the pickups parked at the dock.

"I'll come back later and drive it home," Dad said.

"Where will we put the hay?" asked Pru. "And Velvet?" Then she looked at her smiling father. "Is that what the shed behind your shop is for?"

"Yup. We were sure you'd ask why I was building it."

"I thought it was for more lobstering gear. Was I ever dumb!" Pru gave him a one-armed hug. "I'm glad I didn't guess. Can I ride Velvet now?"

"Not until he's used to his new home," her mom said. "But you can lead him back to school."

"I know how. I had a horse when I was growing up." Miss Sparling showed Pru how to hold the lead rope and walk to one side so the pony would not step on her feet. At school she helped Pru tie the pony to a tree, and then they went inside for cake.

Pru opened her presents. Max and Doug had painted rocks with funny faces. Hannah gave Pru her old Barbie doll. Harry had carved her a toy lobster boat, and Nicholas had made her a journal.

Pru opened Miss Sparling's gift last. It was a book on horse care. "You knew!"

"Well, your parents had to tell me, so I could fake that field trip."

"How old were you when you got your horse?"

"I was eleven, and I got a quarter horse," said the teacher. "I rode in horse shows until I went away to college."

"What was his name?"

"Raffles. I still miss him, and I miss riding. I'll

help you with the pony, if you want. You'll need riding lessons." She took an envelope off her desk.
"Before I forget, we have one more surprise. A letter
from Clara Hall."

Miss Sparling read the letter out loud:

Dear Seal Island School,
I showed your letter to my class. They didn't
believe I sent a letter in a bottle. I told them
they didn't have enough imagination. My
great-grandmother lived on Seal Island. Her
daughter drowned there. She fell off the
rocks. She was six years old.
Clara

"I never climb on high rocks," Max said.

"Me neither," said Doug. "Even to look for
feathers."

"That was a long time ago," Pru added quickly.
She didn't want her teacher to think bad things happened on the island. She hurried over to the table,
cut another piece of cake, and wrapped it in a nap-
kin. "For supper," she said to Miss Sparling. Then she
helped pick up the plates and spoons.

"Thank you, everybody." Pru put her presents in her backpack. "This is my best birthday ever."

Outside, Pru freed the pony's lead rope, and she and her parents started home. "Bye, Velvet," Miss Sparling called from the schoolhouse door.

I have a dog, a gerbil, and a pony, Pru thought. It isn't fair that Miss Sparling doesn't have any pets at all. I want to get her *something*. But what?

24

CHAPTER FOUR

A Dime at a Time

On Saturday morning Pru left home with Schooner to collect more bottles and cans. For every one she took to the general store, she got a dime. Since her birthday last month she had saved $16.70. But it wasn't anywhere near enough for her new idea. She wanted to buy Miss Sparling a dog.

The March sun had melted the ice from the pond near her house. Hockey was over for the winter. No more practices. Now gray-backed gulls splashed in the water and swam in rippling circles.

Pru stopped first at the library and checked out another book on ponies. She had finished the book that Miss Sparling had given her. Ponies, she learned, took much more work than gerbils or dogs. Every day Velvet needed hay and water, and Pru had to shovel manure from the shed onto the compost pile. But Velvet was gentle and well-behaved, and Pru wasn't afraid anymore to pick up his feet and clean his hooves. Miss Sparling had taught her how to bridle and saddle him. "You're lucky the tack came with him," she had said. "Saddles cost a lot to buy new." Pru could ride him safely now at a walk.

She climbed the path to Nicholas's gray-shingled house and knocked on the front door.

"Come in," his mother called. When Pru opened the door, she was in the hall brushing Picasso, the dog. She had long braids, brown as Picasso's coat. "Nicholas is writing in his journal."

Nicholas sat at the dining room table, which was covered with books and papers. "I'm writing about New York," he told Pru. "If I were home, I could be at the Museum of Natural History today seeing you-know-what."

"There's natural history outside," his dad said. "Just open the door."

"Not dinosaurs."

"Want to help me today?" asked Pru. "I'm collecting bottles again. For the dog."

"A teacher's pet? That's a joke. Get it?"

"Not funny. If she has a dog, maybe she'll stay."

"I seriously doubt it." But Nicholas piled empty bottles and cans from the kitchen recycling bin into Pru's wagon, and they walked to the next house where Mr. and Mrs. Bowdoin lived.

"Good morning," said Pru. Mrs. Bowdoin was sweeping her porch. "Do you have any cans we can return? We're saving for a surprise for Miss Sparling."

"That's nice, dear. I won't breathe a word." Mrs. Bowdoin went to her toolshed and came back with two bulging bags.

"Thank you very much," Nicholas said. The next house belonged to Mr. Clarke. They went to the back door.

"Collectin' again, huh?" Mr. Clarke lived alone except for his seven cats. He drank a lot of soda.

"You're my best stop." Pru took his box of cans

and loaded it on the wagon. "Thanks!"

By the time Pru and Nicholas got to the store, the wagon was full. "I count fifty-one," said Mr. Farnum, the storekeeper. "That's five dollars and ten cents."

"That makes twenty-one dollars and eighty cents so far." Pru liked to do addition in her head. "How much do Newfoundland dogs cost?"

"Well, I reckon you could save enough in a year."

"A year! That's too long." Pru shook her head. She stepped back and bumped a carton of dog food next to the counter.

"Be careful! Don't trip over that stuff," Mr. Farnum warned.

Pru looked around at the open boxes of soup, crackers, and peanut butter in the aisles. "How come there are so many today?"

"Unpacking them hurts my back." Mr. Farnum walked slowly from behind the register. "I'm gettin' old."

"I could help," Pru said. "After school."

"Better ask your folks," said Mr. Farnum. "I'd be glad for your company."

"Me, too?" asked Nicholas. "I'm good at organiz-ing."

"You, too. And I'll pay you both a little something."

"Wow! Thanks!" Pru said.

"My first paying position." Nicholas grinned as they left the store. "My parents will be impressed."

"See?" said Pru. "Mr. Farnum's nice. I bet that wouldn't happen in New York."

"My deli gives kids free licorice." Nicholas picked up a candy wrapper and dropped it in the litter barrel. "But I can't go there by myself. It's not safe like here."

They stopped next door at the post office. "Any mail for me today?" Pru asked Mr. Smith, the postmaster. She and Clara now wrote regularly back and forth. Clara couldn't wait to see Velvet and had asked her father to bring her to Seal Island in his lobster boat. But today her letter said:

The engine on our lobster boat broke. We can't come until my dad fixes it. My sister is a pest. She is NOT coming. She put the cat in the clothes dryer. Mom heard it meow and found it.

Pru read the letter to Nicholas.

"I'm glad I'm an only child," he said.

"Why don't you keep the money until we have enough?" Outside the post office, Pru handed the $5.10 to Nicholas. "You've got that secret drawer in your desk. We can count it together every Saturday."

Nicholas folded the dollar bills around the dime and stuffed them in his back pocket.

"After we have the money," Pru went on, "how will we find the dog?"

"Maybe advertise in the *Ellsworth News*?" Nicholas read the newspaper ads, looking for base-ball cards to buy for his collection. "We get it every week."

"Is there a section for dogs?"

"Dogs, cats, horses, everything."

Pru imagined what she might write: "Wanted: Friendly Newfoundland, secondhand, cheap."

"I bet it's hard to find Newfoundlands," Nicholas said. "Have you ever seen one?"

"No, but someone in Maine must have one." They stopped at the path to Nicholas's house.

"Thanks for helping so much," said Pru. "I wish you'd stay on Seal Island."

"I'm getting used to it," said Nicholas, "but when

school's out, my mom and dad have to go back to their jobs."

"Can you get money for poems?" Pru knew Nicholas's father wrote poetry.

"Not much," said Nicholas. "My dad's a teacher, too. My mom has a studio and sells her paintings."

"When you leave," said Pru, "there will only be five kids in the school."

"Four," said Nicholas. "Hannah goes ashore next year for seventh grade. Remember?"

"You're right." Pru did not like to think of losing two of her friends. "Four won't be as much fun."

"Maybe the school will have to close," said Nicholas.

"That's a terrible thing to say!" Pru felt like hitting Nicholas. "Every place has to have a school. It's—" She stopped.

"Compulsory?" asked Nicholas. "Yeah, but maybe not on islands where there aren't enough kids."

CHAPTER FIVE

Squeak, Meow, Chomp

A flock of birds landed on the feeder in the school-yard. They began to eat the oranges Doug and Max had put there.

"Here come the orioles," Pru announced. It was April and spring migration time.

"Maybe they're here for pet day." Miss Sparling cleared a space before her desk. "Keep tight hold of your animals. When it's your turn, please stand here for your report."

Everyone had gone home at lunchtime and come back with a pet to show the class. The dogs pulled at their leashes and growled at strange noises that came from inside the boxes on the floor. One box squeaked, another meowed, and in another something gnawed and chomped at the cardboard, trying to eat its way out.

"Quiet, everyone! And be careful! No close encounters." Miss Sparling tapped Max on the shoulder. "You're first. Please begin."

Max led his ferret to the front of the room. It had on a blue-and-white striped harness with a collar to match. "A ferret belongs to the weasel family," he said. "Like the skunk."

"Phew!" said Harry. "It stinks."

"No interrupting, please," said Miss Sparling.

"Ferocious likes to hide," Max said. "He climbs into my dad's fishing boots and my bed. That's why I put a bell on his collar. So I can find him."

"What does he eat?" Miss Sparling asked.

"He loves raisins. Once he ate a mouse."

"I hope he doesn't eat rabbits," said Miss Sparling. Everyone laughed. "Like our next pet."

"My rabbit is a Black Dutch," Doug said. The rabbit jumped out of his arms and ran under Miss Sparling's desk. "It likes to eat rabbit pellets." He tried to catch it. "My dad made a wire cage that has holes for all the rabbit poop to go through." The rabbit hopped away.

"Thank you, Doug." Miss Sparling smiled. "Put it in the box now."

Doug grabbed the rabbit just as it reached the art shelf and began to chew on a box of crayons.

Harry untied his dog, Snuffles, from a chair. "He's a mix of beagle and German shepherd." Snuffles began to shake, and Harry patted his head to calm him. "He likes to go rowing. I take him out in my dory."

"I saw you," said Max. "How come he wears a life preserver? Can't he swim?"

"I don't know. He won't go in the water."

Just then Snuffles peed on the floor.

"Gross!" Hannah cried. "Isn't your dog house-broken?"

"Of course! No fair making fun of him! He's just scared." He got a paper towel and wiped up the puddle.

Pru tried not to laugh.

"Cats never do that!" Hannah held her nose.

"Stay in your seats, please." Miss Sparling clapped her hands for attention. "The show's not over."

Nicholas was next. "Picasso is named after a famous painter," he said about his dog. "Pablo Picasso. He lived in Spain. All dogs are descended from wolves," Nicholas went on. "Picasso can smell much better than people can. He has forty-two teeth."

Then it was Hannah's turn. She carried a box to the front of the room and lifted out her pet. Picasso barked at the cat, who hissed at him.

"Maine coon cats are smart," said Hannah. "Mine likes to look at books. Once I read her *The Cat in the Hat*."

Pru was last. "May I bring my pet in?" she asked with a smile.

"Can he climb stairs?" asked Miss Sparling.

"Just joking. C'mon out, everybody."

Velvet waited by the railing, his coat brushed smooth and shiny. "Velvet is twelve hands high," Pru began. "A hand is four inches. If you feed ponies too much, they can get colic and die." Velvet swished his long, black tail and sneezed.

Pru lifted Velvet's front foot. "I clean his feet with a hoof pick. He's a grade pony. That means he isn't pure Welsh or Shetland or anything. Just a mix."

They took turns riding Velvet around the schoolyard.

"Now for the prizes." Miss Sparling led them back inside and pinned a blue ribbon on each pet owner. "Good reports! Next year you can do it again."

"Does she mean she'll be here to help us?" Pru asked Nicholas as they put on their backpacks and got ready to leave.

"It's a mystery," said Nicholas.

Pru rode Velvet home and then they walked to the store with Picasso. So far they had earned twenty-five dollars working for Mr. Farnum. Each Saturday they added to their recycling money. "There's sixty-five dollars and ten cents now in the secret drawer," Nicholas reported.

"We'd better collect more bottles," said Pru. "And then when the tourists come, we can make shell sculptures and sell them."

"But tourists mean summer's almost here. And I have to leave."

"Won't you be glad?" asked Pru. "You miss New York."

"I'm not sure anymore."

"My parents asked Mr. Bowdoin about the school staying open next year," Pru said. "He's on the school board."

"What did he say?"

"There have to be at least five kids to afford a teacher." Pru waved to Mr. Clarke who was drinking a can of soda in front of the post office.

"Maybe you could come to New York and live with us," Nicholas offered.

"No way!" Pru shook her head. "I'd never leave Seal Island. Though it's nice of you to invite me," she added quickly.

Miss Sparling came into the store while they were stacking cans on the shelves.

"Does the Saturday boat start soon?" she asked Mr. Farnum. "I'll be glad to go ashore."

Pru looked at Nicholas. "See?" he whispered. "What did I tell you?"

"Going to visit your sister in Portland?" Mr. Farnum asked.

"Does she have a dog?" Pru walked up to her teacher.

"No. Why do you ask?"

"If she did, I thought maybe she could give it to you. For company. You didn't get that Newfoundland."

Miss Sparling laughed. "I haven't saved enough money yet." She paid for her groceries. "What are you and Nicholas saving for with all this work you're doing?"

"A boa constrictor." Pru said the first thing that popped into her head.

Miss Sparling looked surprised. "Do your parents know?"

"Gotta get to work." Pru hurried back to her box of cans.

"That was close," Nicholas said after Miss Sparling left the store. "You'd better watch it."

"It would spoil everything if she found out." Pru sighed.

"If the school closes, it won't matter whether she has a dog or not."

"If the school closes, Mom says I'll have to live with my grandmother in Rockland and go to school there."

"I'd hate that," said Nicholas.

"Me, too."

CHAPTER SIX

Good News and Bad

Gray fog wrapped the island in a soft blanket. The foghorn boomed from the jetty at the harbor entrance. "Look out! Look out!" it seemed to say, warning boats away from the rocks, hidden now and dangerous.

Pru stepped outdoors and thought of her father, out in the bad weather hauling traps. Fog droplets wet her face. The air smelled of salt. Thump! Thump! She heard Velvet kick the sides of his stall, a sign he was hungry.

"I just wrote a letter to Clara," Pru said to Velvet

41

as she shook hay into the manger. "Maybe she knows someone who has a Newfoundland for sale."

Velvet pricked up his ears and then dropped his head to eat. "I told her that we've got eighty-nine dollars now." Velvet stopped chewing and nudged Pru with his nose. "You think that's enough, do you?" She filled his water bucket, gave him a hug, and went back in the house.

"I've finished my newspaper article on Mr. Farnum and the general store," Mom said. He had been the storekeeper ever since she was a little girl and candy bars cost ten cents. "When you get back from recycling, will you take it to the post office?"

"Sure. I'll ride Velvet. He needs exercise." Pru loaded the wheelbarrow with glass, plastic, and cardboard and started for the dock. Monday the boat would carry it all inshore.

"Hi, Mrs. Bowdoin." Pru's neighbor was raking the mulch from her flower beds.

"Spring's come at last," Mrs. Bowdoin said.

Pru felt the warm sun behind the fog. She loved this time of year. Green grass, orioles, and daffodils. She sorted the recycling into bins and pushed the empty wheelbarrow back home.

She led Velvet out of his stall and fit the bit into his mouth and the bridle over his ears. So far she'd had eight riding lessons. She could trot now without falling off. "I'll ride bareback today," she said to her mother. "I can practice later with the saddle." Max and Doug waved from the beach as she and Velvet walked by.

At the post office Pru looped Velvet's reins to a railing and poked her mail through the drop slot inside the tiny white building.

"Is this another letter from your pen pal?" Mr. Smith asked. He handed Pru an envelope covered with pony stickers. "When are we going to meet her?"

Pru tore open the envelope and read the few lines. "Great!" she said. "The boat's fixed and she'll come as soon as it's calm and there's no fog. The boat's named the *Clara H*. After her."

"Pretty special to have a boat named for you," Mr. Smith said.

The front door creaked open and closed. Miss Sparling came in with an armload of boxes.

"Clara's coming!" Pru told her. "I can hardly wait."

"If she comes on a school day, we'll have a party for her."

"If she doesn't, I'll bring her to your house." Pru was already imagining what she would do to make Clara's visit perfect. What favorite places would they visit? She felt a little scared, too. Would they like each other?

"Can you help me with these boxes?" Miss Sparling asked.

"Why are there so many?" Pru started across the room.

"I'm cleaning house."

Pru stopped halfway. "Why?"

"It's spring. I'm sending things to my sister in Portland."

"How come?" Pru was sure now that Miss Sparling was moving.

"Until I decide what to do with them."

44

Pru couldn't say another word. She handed the boxes one by one to the postmaster to weigh. They were heavy. Miss Sparling must be getting rid of *everything*.

Pru felt awful now. Wait until Nicholas heard about the packages. But maybe he wouldn't even care. He was going back to New York.

She said good-bye, mounted Velvet, and rode to Nicholas's house. This time she trotted.

GONE TO THE LIGHTHOUSE. Nicholas liked to leave messages on the front door in case anyone came to see him while he was out. Pru turned Velvet up the narrow path to the lighthouse. Wispy ribbons of fog wound past her and floated away. When she reached the top, the fog had lifted and the sky was blue as the sea. She could see Greenbush Island far away to the west. Beyond, out of sight, was Cranberry Cove.

"Hi, Pru." Nicholas's mom had set up her easel next to the lighthouse. "Want to paint with us?"

"I'm drawing dinosaurs." Nicholas sat on the ground with a pencil and his journal. Picasso gnawed at a crab shell. Pru liked to draw, especially boats and houses, but now she wanted only to tell them her news. "Not now, thanks," she said without even dismounting. "First, the good stuff. Clara's coming soon."

"That's nice," said Nicholas's mom. "Let us know when. We don't want to miss her."

"Is there bad stuff?" Nicholas asked.

Pru felt a tight lump in her stomach. "Miss Sparling's leaving."

"How do you know?" Nicholas put down his journal.

"She's already sending boxes at the post office."

"I don't believe it."

"It's true. I saw her." Pru felt like crying and turned her head away so no one could see her face.

"I've got more bottles for the store," said Nicholas. "That's good news, isn't it?"

"It's too late." Pru nudged Velvet forward with her heels. "I'm going home to tell Mom."

CHAPTER SEVEN

The *Clara H.* Ties Up

Pru rolled out of bed and ran to the window. The waves splashed in the sun. It was Sunday. Clara was coming at last.

The lilac bushes by the front door showed purple buds. May was here, but the mornings were still cool. Pru pulled on a sweater over her T-shirt.

"What's the plan?" her dad asked. He put three blueberry pancakes on her plate. "Will there be a band at the dock to welcome her?"

"Harry said he'd play his trumpet, but I told him no."

"Wise girl."

"I'm meeting her boat and showing her around."

"Bring her here for lunch," said her mom. "We want to see the famous Clara. Bring your other friends, too."

"Thanks!"

"Maybe Nicholas's parents want to come." Dad poured syrup on his pancakes. "We'll ask them."

"How about the governor?" Mom asked.

"Invite the president!" Pru laughed.

After breakfast Pru saddled Velvet and rode to the dock. Gulls called overhead and the lobster boats dipped and bobbed at their moorings. Mr. Bowdoin waved from his boat, where he was washing the deck.

"We'll come with the outgoing tide," Clara had written. "About nine o'clock. And go back when it turns."

The lobster boat cut through the water. *Clara H.*, it said on the side. Its dory skimmed behind, held fast with a long line.

"There's her name, just like she wrote," Pru said as she slid off Velvet. A girl with red hair waved from the stern. Pru waved back. She watched Mr. Hall secure the boat to a mooring in the harbor. Then Clara and her father climbed into the dory and rowed ashore.

"Hi!" Clara smiled and waved again. She scrambled out of the dory onto the dock. "Are you Pru?"

Pru nodded. "I thought you'd never get here."

"Safe seas and clear skies today." Mr. Hall shook Pru's hand. "We're mighty glad." His hands were big and strong and his cheeks tanned. Like Dad's, thought Pru.

"I *know* this is Velvet." Clara walked around the pony, who tried to nibble her sleeve. "He's just like you told me."

Pru decided right away that she liked Clara. "Everyone wants to meet you."

"I'm going to Mr. Bowdoin's house," said Mr. Hall. "To talk lobstering. See you back here at one o'clock."

"Dad and Mr. Bowdoin are old friends," Clara explained after her father had left. "Can I pat Velvet?"

"You can ride him." Pru took Clara's pack and then helped her on Velvet's back.

"We saw your boat come in." Doug ran up to them.

"I brought my ferret," Max said. "You can hold it."

"Uh . . . maybe later." Clara slid her feet into the stirrups. "But thanks."

"I'm taking her around the island." Pru held the reins. "Want to come?"

"Sure," Doug said.

Pru walked Velvet up the road. Clara held on to the front of the saddle. Mr. Bowdoin's son waved from the inn where he was painting the porch. "He's getting ready for the tourists," Pru explained.

"It's the same in Cranberry Cove. My dad's helping paint the lighthouse."

"Want to go to our school first?" asked Pru.

"I want to see everything."

"It's got two rooms," said Max.

"We're in one," Doug said. "The other is for supplies."

"And the toilets," Max added.

In the schoolyard, Pru gave the reins to Doug to hold and Clara slid off Velvet. "Riding was fun. Velvet isn't scary at all."

"Is it always unlocked?" asked Clara as Pru pushed open the door.

"Yup. No one would steal anything."

Clara looked at the five desks and the pictures and maps on the wall. "It's cozy. But it sure is tiny. Where do you have gym?"

"Outdoors," said Pru. "Unless it's raining."

"Help!" Doug called. "Velvet's eating my sneaker!"

"It's okay." Pru hurried back outside. "He likes to smell things."

"Your sneakers smell, all right," Max said. "Like dead fish."

"Miss Sparling's asked us over next." Pru mounted Velvet this time and led everyone along the road. Max ran into his house to leave Ferocious and came out with four Popsicles.

After a few moments they rounded a turn and the road narrowed. Now they went single file.

"That's where she lives." Pru pointed to a small,

gray house. Red and yellow lobster buoys hung beside the back door. Pru tied Velvet to the porch rail and knocked. She heard her teacher's footsteps cross the kitchen.

"Hello, everyone," said Miss Sparling. "Welcome to Seal Island, Clara! I'm glad to meet the remarkable letter writer at last."

"I was excited when Pru found my bottle."

"Come in. I've baked cinnamon rolls." They sat down at the kitchen table.

"You want a dog?" Clara asked.

"Who told you that?" Miss Sparling turned toward Pru with a smile. "Never mind, I can guess."

Why do you want it if you're leaving, Pru thought. But she didn't say anything. Then she held her breath, afraid Clara would say something about the money. But Clara talked instead about her cat, Clam.

"I like to eat clams," Doug said. "Even the necks."

"Yuck!" said Max. "Necks taste like Play-Doh."

"How big is your third grade?" Miss Sparling asked Clara.

"Sixteen. It's third and fourth together. They want to come here."

"What about a class trip sometime?"

"Yeah!" said Doug. "You could collect feathers."

"Maybe you could stay overnight," Pru said.

"Here's something to remember us by." Miss Sparling gave Clara a tiny lobster buoy on a string. "We hope you'll visit again soon."

"Thank you." Clara hung the buoy around her neck. "I like it here."

Miss Sparling walked with them to the door.

"She's really nice," Clara said as she climbed on the pony again.

"If she goes away, I don't know what we'll do with the dog money." Pru took the reins. Doug and Max ran ahead.

"Maybe you can give her a dog as a good-bye present. My dad says there's a place in Ellsworth where they recycle dogs."

"How can you do that?" asked Pru.

"They save purebreds when people move and can't take them. Instead of sending them to the Humane Society."

"Do they actually give you the dogs?" Pru suddenly imagined getting a free Newfoundland. It sounded too good to be true. With the money she and Nicholas had saved they could buy one of those cushiony, round dog beds from the L. L. Bean catalog or a special bowl with the dog's name on it. Pru had always wanted a dog bed for Schooner. Miss Sparling would love one, Pru was sure.

"I don't know. Ask my dad when we go back to the dock."

Pru did not want to think about good-bye presents. Much better were presents that stayed on Seal Island with the people you liked. She didn't know what to do now. "That's my house. The white one with the green door."

"Can we trot the rest of the way?" Clara asked. "I think I can do it." Pru jogged forward, and Velvet broke into a slow trot.

"Hi!" Harry ran from behind Velvet's shed. "I'm practicing fast starts."

"We got here early." Hannah stepped out the front door. "I was helping your mom."

Pru introduced them to Clara.

"We're coming with you into the woods." Harry caught his breath.

"To show you our most favorite place," said Hannah.

"Where's that?"

"It's a surprise," Doug said.

Pru took Velvet's bridle and saddle off and closed him in the stall. Then they walked along the road toward the beginning of the trail. They passed a big house with peeling white paint and a lawn full of weeds. On the roof was a cupola with windows.

"That looks like my great-grandmother's house," said Clara. "My dad showed me pictures. From that tower she could see the boats come into the harbor."

"We think it's spooky." Hannah led them to a window.

"There're cobwebs." Max peered in. "And dead mice."

"It belongs to my uncle," said Clara, "but he lives in Alaska and almost never comes. My dad wants to buy it. Then we could rent it to summer people or use it weekends."

"Could you?" Pru asked. "That would be great! When?"

"I don't know." Clara shook her head. "My dad's looking for work. The fishing isn't so good around home. Not enough lobsters."

"There's still a lot of them here," said Harry.

In the woods the trees rose around them, tall and green. "It's like walking in a tunnel," Clara said. The path was soft with pine needles and moss.

"What are those?" Clara pointed to little houses made of twigs on the forest floor.

"Fairy houses," said Doug. "We build them."

"You put a penny in and the fairies grant your wish," Hannah explained.

Pru took six pennies from her pocket and gave one to each of her friends. "Let's make a wish. Let's wish Clara will come back soon."

"I'll wish that," said Clara.

"Me, too," said Doug and Max.

"I'm wishing for a new bike," said Harry.

"I wish I won't be homesick next year when I go ashore to school." Hannah rubbed her penny on her shirttail to make it shine.

They set their pennies on the ground underneath the stick roofs.

"Do the wishes ever come true?" Clara asked.

"I got my wish for a ferret," said Max.

"I got my gerbil." Pru hesitated. "Actually, I saved my allowance for it."

They turned right at a trail marker and started back on another path.

"Nicholas wants to meet you," said Harry. "He's that kid from New York."

"I remember his big words." Clara followed Harry and Pru out of the woods into the sun. Nicholas was sitting on his front porch with Picasso.

"Hi!" Nicholas stared at Clara. "You look different than I thought."

"What did you expect?"

"A lady pirate, who sent messages in bottles."

"He reads a lot," said Pru.

"I like people with imagination." Clara sat down beside him.

"Want to hear my journal?" asked Nicholas.

"Not now," Harry said. "We want to make a good impression on Clara."

"I'd like it," said Clara. "Writing's my favorite subject."

"New York is full of people and cars and dirt," Nicholas read. "Seal Island is clean and the wind whistles. New York is exciting. Seal Island is boring sometimes. I'll miss the lighthouse and the foghorn. Everyone here is my friend."

"That's enough." Pru stopped him. She didn't want to hear another word about people leaving. "Get up!" She grabbed Nicholas's hand. "I've decided on a new plan. We need to find Clara's dad fast."

CHAPTER EIGHT

The Unexpected Visitor

The schoolhouse doors and windows stood open to the warm wind off the sea. In the back room Pru pulled the long bell rope. Twenty dongs across the island. "Last day," it donged. "Last day."

She watched the front room fill with families for the end-of-year celebration. Hannah's grandparents had come from the mainland and sat down next to Mr. Farnum. He waved to Pru as she pushed her way through the crowd. "How's my helper? Couldn't have made it through the spring without you."

"Mom said you might sell the store." Pru looked at Mr. Farnum's kind, old face. "What will happen to it?"

"I reckon it will keep goin' without me."

"But you can't leave!" Pru could not imagine the island without the storekeeper.

"Not a chance. I'm staying right next door. Maybe now I'll have time to go fishin'."

"The ferry's at the dock." Captain Hill made his way over to Pru. "With you-know-what aboard. I haven't said a word." Pru put her finger to her lips and sat down. Her parents were late. She and Nicholas knew why, but they weren't telling anybody. She tapped her feet on the floor and stood up, looked around, and sat down three times. Nicholas and his parents waved from the first row.

Miss Sparling walked to the front of the room in her blue dress with the yellow flowers. She touched the bouquet of purple lupine on her desk and winked at Pru. Pru had picked the flowers that morning. The celebration was about to begin.

Hannah and Harry handed out the programs, which they had copied in their best writing. Miss Sparling led everyone in "My Country, 'Tis of Thee," just the way she did most school mornings. But this morning, Pru got a lump in her throat. She swallowed it and kept singing.

The children came forward to get their report cards. Hannah was last. Miss Sparling gave her a diploma in a velvet box. "This is to certify," she read, "that Hannah Spencer has completed the sixth grade at Seal Island School, Seal Island, Maine. She is now promoted to the seventh grade."

"Thank you." Hannah turned red as a lobster.

Everyone clapped.

Mr. Bowdoin stood up next. "As chairman of the school board, I want to thank you for your support this year. We have a fine school and you have all made it that way."

Pru knew what was coming next. The bad news.

Mr. Bowdoin went on. "Most of all, I want to thank our teacher, Miss Sparling. She has done a terrific job."

"Hear! Hear!" cried Nicholas's father.

"You will want to know—" Mr. Bowdoin stopped to clear his throat.

For goodness' sake, hurry up, thought Pru.

"We'll have two more students," he went on. "The

Hall family is coming to live in the white house. Joe Hall was here just yesterday. He wanted to be sure the school would be open. I told him yes."

Clara was moving to Seal Island! That was a surprise. Pru wasn't expecting good news. But who would be the teacher? The front door shut with a bang. Pru's parents burst into the room.

Mr. Bowdoin tried to speak. But everybody was pointing at the Stanleys and talking. Pru's father had a huge, hairy animal on a leash. A Newfoundland. It was almost as big as Velvet.

"Quiet, please," Mr. Bowdoin said in a louder voice. "We have another announcement."

Pru looked at Nicholas. He made a thumbs-up sign.

"We wanted to give Miss Sparling a present to show our appreciation. Pru Stanley told us what she wanted. With help from Pru and Nicholas we found it." Mr. Bowdoin took the leash from Pru's father and presented it with a bow to Miss Sparling.

"He's magnificent!" Miss Sparling knelt in front of the dog who tried to put his paws on her shoulders. "Where did you find him?"

"I called the recycling place." Pru jumped up again. "Clara and her dad went and got him in Ellsworth. His name is Gander."

"The dog was not free," Mr. Bowdoin explained. "Pru and Nicholas earned most of the money for him. They deserve a hand."

Everyone stamped and whistled.

"Now, our last announcement. Miss Sparling has—" Mr. Bowdoin pushed his glasses higher on his nose.

Get it over with, thought Pru.

"Miss Sparling has agreed to come back and teach—"

Pru did not wait for him to finish. "Hooray!" She jumped up and down. "Hooray!" She waved her arms in the air.

Everybody laughed. Then they cheered and clapped for Miss Sparling. "Thank you," she said with a smile.

"We have something to say, too." Nicholas's father turned to the room of people. "My wife and I are going to buy the general store from Mr. Farnum and stay on the island."

I can't believe what's happening, thought Pru. Nicholas never told me that. She clapped until her hands hurt.

"That is the end of our program." Mr. Bowdoin took off his glasses and slid them into his pocket. "You are all invited to lunch outdoors. The dads made a special meal."

Pru followed everyone into the yard. People crowded around Miss Sparling. Did she like the dog? Pru wondered. Maybe it wasn't as exciting as getting a puppy. Gander was three years old. His family had moved to South America.

"Pru, come here!" Miss Sparling gave her a hug. "I love him. He's perfect." Gander wagged his plumy tail and licked Miss Sparling's shoe. "I know how hard you worked."

"Nicholas, too," said Pru. "We stacked a lot of cans."

"Gander can have his very own room. I'm buying the little house I'm renting. Andy Taylor is going to help me fix it up." Andy had gone away to college and come back to work on the island as a carpenter.

"I was sure you were leaving." Pru took a big swal-

65

low of lemonade. The excitement made her thirsty. "All those packages you mailed."

"I thought I was leaving, too. I was homesick at first, and then really lonesome, but you all changed my mind."

Pru's parents crossed the yard to shake Miss Sparling's hand. "Come by and see us any time you want company," Mom said.

"Nice job, Pru." Her father gave her a kiss.

"I was afraid you would see the dog before Mom and Dad got here."

"I didn't have a clue," said Miss Sparling.

"Captain Hill kept him below deck," Mom said. "When everyone was inside the school, we went to the boat and got him."

"Let's find Nicholas," Dad said. "I want to congratulate him, too." They walked to the flagpole where Nicholas and his parents stood talking to Mr. Farnum.

"We heard rumors, but we never dreamed you'd do it." Pru's mother greeted Nicholas's parents.

"I'll be helpin' them for a while," said Mr. Farnum.

"You're one reason we're staying, Pru." Nicholas's father took a bite of lobster salad. "You're the finest kind."

Nicholas grinned. "Were you surprised about the store? I wanted to keep it a secret."

"I still can't believe it," Pru said.

"This time Mom and Dad told me everything," Nicholas explained. "I only agreed today—after much deliberation. Besides, they promised I could go back to New York at least twice a year."

"I'm glad you're staying," Pru said. They crossed the yard to Gander. Harry and Hannah were trying to guess the dog's height.

"If he stood on his hind legs, he'd be as tall as I am," Hannah said.

"This canine definitely has class." Nicholas tossed a fried clam to Gander, who caught it in his mouth.

"Do you suppose he can swim?" Harry looked at Gander's big legs. "Now that it's summer, maybe he can teach Snuffles."

"Time to start making shell sculptures," said Pru.

"Why do we need the money?" Nicholas asked.

"We don't have to buy a dog anymore."

"Maybe we can save it for a trip to New York. You can show me that museum with the dinosaurs."

"Superexcellent! I'll show you the mummies, too."

"Take me!" Max ran up to them.

"And me!" Doug was right behind him. "Where are you going?"

"We're going to New York," Nicholas said.

"We'll all go," said Pru. "Miss Sparling, too." She and Nicholas swapped high fives. "Let's start looking for shells right after lunch."